SMALL ALTARS

SMALL ALTARS

Justin Gardiner

TUPELO PRESS

Library of Congress Cataloging-in-Publication data available upon request.
ISBN-13: 978-1-961209-06-0

Cover and text design by Allison O'Keefe
Cover illustration by Colin Sutherland. Used by permission of the artist.

First paperback edition April 2024

Tupelo Press
P.O. Box 1767
North Adams, Massachusetts 01247
(413) 664-9611 / Fax: (413) 664-9711
editor@tupelopress.org / www.tupelopress.org

Tupelo Press is an award-winning independent literary press that publishes fine fiction, non-fiction, and poetry in books that are a joy to hold as well as read. Tupelo Press is a registered 501(c)(3) nonprofit organization, and we rely on public support to carry out our mission of publishing extraordinary work that may be outside the realm of the large commercial publishers. Financial donations are welcome and are tax deductible.

This project is supported in part by the National Endowment for the Arts

For my parents—
for all they've done

Then again, that's the hero gig—part of the journey is the end.

—Tony Stark, *Avengers: Endgame*

My brother plays the piano. A video loop displayed on a wide screen. We see him in profile: a black T-shirt and thinning hair, seated at an old scarred Bechstein. A heavy man at the time, soft. You would expect his plump fingers to struggle at finding all the right notes, but they don't—at least not to my untrained ear. His posture is surprisingly upright, his eyes fixed intently on the sheet music before him, for this is his chance to be taken seriously—by others, by himself. He is playing Debussy's *Clair de Lune*—the poet's song, though I do not know this yet. Surely, by now, I have heard him play this piece a hundred times, but for some reason I have never bothered to look it up. Behind my brother is a light green gymnasium wall—the school and center where he works. This is their annual awards banquet, and they have invited him, again, to play. In preparation for this day, my brother has been practicing for weeks, for years, for his entire life. A door creaks open somewhere behind him, as my brother lifts his hands, slowly, from the last drawn-out notes. Then he turns toward the camera, where our father sits, and he smiles.

There is some commotion. I turn back to the solemn room. My brother's best friend, who I have only just met, is having one of her seizures. Chairs and a table are pushed clear; people huddle close by. On the screen behind me, my brother begins playing his next song. The shirt of his friend has lifted up, exposing her pale stomach, as she wriggles helplessly on the floor. Her young daughter, kneeling beside her, reaches over and pulls the shirt back into place.

We had decided to call this event a "celebration," but make no mistake: this is about death.

"I don't know if you are ever going to see these," Tony Stark begins, after flicking on the recorder built into his half-ruined mask. "Oxygen will run out tomorrow morning, and that will be it." Sad orchestral backing. His battered spaceship has been drifting through outer space for three weeks, though his crooked good looks—his infallible Hollywood face—shows only a hint of stubble. "Dead in the water," he laments to his beautiful wife back home, "a thousand light years away from the nearest 7-11." His only companion onboard is a bald, blue mechanical lady—her robot voice sounding like a geriatric Kathleen Turner. Later on, there will be a talking raccoon. I only know the A-list superheroes from the comic books of our youth. Tony Stark bends over to click off the recorder, then slumps lifelessly to the floor.

Beside me sits my brother. Though we don't know it yet, this will be the last movie we ever watch together. Of course, there have been plenty of signs. The tumor in his right lung so large now that he couldn't walk across the cinema parking lot without stopping for a rest. Still, in this moment, I have no idea how seriously he is considering his own end, as he looks up intently at the glowing screen. My brother knows that Tony Stark is not actually dead. He knows this because he has already seen this movie several times before, and because that is not how superhero movies work. A blinding light and Iron Man is saved, transported safely back down to earth.

This is, however, only a brief reprieve. The Marvel industry gods have spoken—one last box office hit before the actor's contract is up, and then the iron mask will be put finally to rest. Yet over these last three intervening hours, he will save the whole world.

We had, I think, a near perfect childhood. Our tree-lined street—just off Happy Lane—was a haven of rotating games: ball-tag, water balloon fights, Kick the Can. There was the small network of trails to Bond Park—a maze of spindly apple trees and blackberry bramble where we would build our endlessly falling down forts. There was the cul-de-sac where the Montoya brothers lived, four and six years our elders—indifferent to us for the most part, though also a looming threat of menace, easily provoked by a well-timed heckle or prank. And there was the alleyway bike path, lined by wooden fencing, that opened out into the adjoining neighborhood—a five-minute walk at most, but almost a half hour by car—so it always seemed a separate world to us, free of the consequences and oversight of our parents, where we could linger until the last summer tendrils of dusk.

But now—in this memory—we are seated inside at our large dining room table, where all our stories start. Probably it is raining again, that interminable gray drizzle of a standard northwest childhood. Or perhaps it is one of those rare, blessed snow days. Our long-soaked clothes left in a heap, our unmittened hands still clenched with the cold as we wait for the hot chocolate to be served. In any case, we are joined by a handful of the neighborhood kids, consumed with fantasy role-playing games.

Sometimes it was *Top Secret*, with its imaginary mob bosses and FBI agents; or it was *Dungeons & Dragons*, with its Tolkien world of elves, wizards, and orcs. Our favorite, however, was always *Marvel Superheroes*. Thor and Captain America. Black Widow and Iron Man and the Incredible Hulk. The names themselves already a demeanor, a troubled past, a boast.

Modules were store-bought adventures, interactive, meticulously planned, so that one player—the Game Master—could oversee the fight-sequences, the dramatic series of events. Over-priced, and each module only playable once, so we took to inventing our own. Doomsday plot lines and improbable rescues. The imagined villains as faceless to me now as the mothers of our childhood friends, but I can still make out perfectly the manners and expressions of their sons seated across from me. Along with my brother— quieter than the rest, thankful just to be included (though he was two years older than us)—finding relief, even then, at pretending to be someone else. And it was up to the Game Master to oversee this tale, to establish who was in need of being helped and who got saved. Though really it was all about setting the odds—our young faces huddled over the table, while one of us rolled the dice.

All superheroes have an origin story. The series of events— most often tragic—that give birth to their powers and lead them into becoming who they are today. Tony Stark, before he became Iron Man, was a millionaire playboy and an ingenious scientist. They say his character was modeled after Howard Hughes, without the crippling neurosis. Telling, which plotlines we remain true to, which details we add and subtract, what we choose to replace.

By the time Stark is a young man, he has already built an empire manufacturing weapons, but then he suffers a severe chest injury during a kidnapping and is only kept alive by a magnetic plate that is installed to keep the shrapnel from reaching his heart. Held captive in a cave, he is ordered to make weapons of mass destruction, but he designs, instead, an iron suit to wage battle with his captors and orchestrate his escape.

My brother was born with a borderline learning disability. He did not excel at sports or school. He never had a girlfriend or finished college or got a decent job. In his twenties, he was diagnosed with paranoid schizophrenia, and much of the fifteen years that followed was wasted away in breakdowns, treatments, a revolving series of doctors and meds.

If this were a Hollywood movie, or even a decent comic book, we could expect, here, a turning: *Then one day it happened, and he became . . .* But in the theater of this life, my brother was only ever cast to play himself. Minor role, thankless task. And so, after a few years where he had kept things mostly together, he contracted a rare form of cancer, and three years later—at the age of forty-four—he died. My brother's story is one of the saddest I know. But much of that comes down to me. My failure to recognize how he could ever be content—happy, even—with what little he had: a job mopping floors; a one-bedroom apartment; years—a whole decade, in fact—when our aging father and mother were his only real friends.

To get to my brother's hospital bed, I cancelled a week of classes, drove an hour and a half to the Atlanta Airport before dawn, caught a connecting flight in Denver and touched down in Oregon late in the afternoon. Our sister and brother-in-law, our niece and nephew, all live in the same town as my brother, within five miles of him, actually. By the time I arrived, Aaron had been in the hospital for close to forty-eight hours—in another forty-eight hours he would be dead—but, apart from our parents, I was the first to visit him. And I don't know what to do with this fact, how not to write it down. Not that this should be misunderstood as any sort of easy virtue. After all, I was the one who moved away, who chose to place that distance between us.

Comic books, also known as floppies, were first popularized in the United States in the 1930s. This Golden Era introduced the archetype of the superhero, including the likes of Batman, Superman, and Wonder Woman. Many of the early storylines were designed, at least in part, to ease young readers' fear of nuclear war, and these first heroes were largely infallible, with good conquering evil at every turn.

Synovial sarcoma is a soft-tissue cancer that accounts for less than 1% of all cancers. The word "synovial" comes from the name of the lining of the joints, while "sarcoma" denotes a tumor made of cancer cells in the bone and soft tissue. It is usually found in teens and young adults.

The Marvel Comic Book Era began in 1961. It helped to revolutionize the genre through developing flawed characters that struggled with inner-demons and self-doubt. X-Men was one of the first series from Marvel. After the addition of Wolverine—perhaps the quintessential anti-hero—in 1975 (the same year as my brother's birth), X-Men became one of the most popular comics of all time.

The cells associated with synovial sarcoma are constituted from genes that have errors in them. These **gene glitches** form over time for unknown reasons and are not passed down through families.

The X-Men were **mutants**, a subspecies of humans who were born with supernatural powers activated by the "X-Gene." Charles Xavier, better known as Professor X, founded a school that recruited mutants from around the world, teaching them to use their powers and live peacefully with humanity.

*Synovial sarcoma starts commonly in the legs or arms. This is a **high-grade tumor**, meaning that it spreads to distant sites in up to 50% of cases. The most common—and most troublesome—location for metastases is the lungs.*

*A **thought balloon** (as opposed to a **speech balloon**) expresses a comic book character's unvoiced thoughts. It is usually shaped like a cloud, with bubbles as a pointer.*

In truth, it was our father who first noticed the tumor, after reaching down to tie one of my brother's shoes. "My God," he thought, "what is this?"

For the last ten years of my brother's life, he worked as a janitor at the Pearl Buck Center, a pre-school designed for children whose parents struggle with cognitive challenges. The center also offers vocational services and day activities for adults with intellectual and developmental disabilities. Five afternoons a week my brother cleaned the classrooms, the teachers' offices, the restrooms and common areas. He had a supervisor and a small group of co-workers who all had their own struggles with mental health. My brother loved going to work, loved seeing his co-workers—perhaps the only genuine friendships of his adult life—and he regretted the long absences he was forced to take near the end, as he recovered from multiple surgeries or intensive rounds of chemo. Beyond the unflagging help and patience of our parents, Pearl Buck played the biggest role in improving the quality of my brother's life. Over the years, our parents got to know some of the teachers and staff at the Center, but I wouldn't meet any of the people my brother loved to talk about until after he was gone.

It is hard to explain my hesitancy toward this. Why, even though I knew where the Center was, I never once stepped inside. Granted, I lived in other states for most of this time, but it wasn't just that, as I came home often enough. I knew full well how important Pearl Buck was to my brother, yet I avoided any direct contact with it. I think I worried, in some way, that the more real the place became for me—the walls of the classrooms, say, or the faces of his troubled friends—the more tenuous it all would become. A job can come to an end, after all. An organization or school can get shut down. Friends can move or fall away. The Pearl Buck Center was no ordinary place for my family, so it was hard to accept it for what it was: just another four-digit address in an aging line of buildings on the far side of town.

The movie flashes forward five years: a memorial for "the Vanished," pods of whales now swimming in the Hudson. The Avengers have failed, they have let everybody down. Half of all living creatures turned to dust with a villain's simple snap. Iron Man has retreated with his family to a private lake in the upstate woods, while Captain America leads a griever's support group in downtown Manhattan. Survivor's guilt as a brief but dramatic segue.

—I can imagine this as another essay entirely: quoting philosophers in place of superheroes, pulling in obscure books instead of Hollywood blockbusters. Yet what would that have to do with the person my brother was?

When we were kids, we would spend full days at the multiplex. We'd each pay a single fare, then sneak into movie after movie, subsisting on popcorn, sweet tarts, and bottomless Cokes. Outside, there was a whole world lying in wait—school and expectations and a hundred small and large failures to come. But the movie—whatever it was— was still playing, so neither of us had to go there yet.

Even in his last better years of mental health, my brother was not an easy person to be around. He was tone deaf to most social cues and norms. He struggled to shave his own face cleanly or to trim his nails. If you came across him for the first time in public, you would know right away that something about him was off. While there was nothing about my brother that was outwardly threatening, you might choose to keep your distance, or give a knowing side glance to whoever you were with. "Heavily medicated" you would likely think, and in this you would be correct. My brother was never bright, but the decades of illness and medications had taken their toll, making him both stranger and simpler.

But if you had spent time with my brother in the last years of his life, he would have made you laugh. Sometimes, intentionally. He was sarcastic and self-deprecating. He liked to kid around with others as well, though never at the expense of kindness. When our whole family got together, he would often get left out of the conversation and grow quiet or sulk. If you gave him a platform to talk, however, he could go on and on. He would retell stories at such painful lengths that whatever it was he had found funny about them got lost. His humor was often forced and obvious, but he loved to laugh. He loved to try and make you laugh.

From the first moment I laid eyes on my brother in that hospital bed I knew he was going to die, and that it would happen soon. All day, in transit—in airport cafes and security checkpoints—I had been preparing myself for just this, yet I was still caught off guard by the fierce certainty of this fact, and how everyone seemed fully aware of it but him. He was eager to talk, but it was hard to understand him at first through his oxygen mask. "Like Darth Vader" he said, pulling off his mask to make sure I caught the joke, though almost immediately the machine beside him started beeping as his oxygen levels plunged. And it wasn't just the sound of the machine, as my brother could hardly manage a full sentence before he would start gasping for breath. The worst part, however, was the violent heaving of his chest—the unnatural way it would rise and fall no matter what he did.

So this is death, I thought to myself; a phenomenon that—up until that point in my life—I had strangely little familiarity with. By then, I had lost each of my grandparents, as well as an uncle—almost all to various forms of cancer—

but I'd seen only one of them during the last week of her life, and by then she was so ready to go that death had seemed merciful; to her, to all of us. But my brother did not want to die—despite all his struggles—and death for him would never come as a mercy.

"When will I get to come home" he kept asking our parents. His hopes, his desires were so simple by that point in time. What he wanted, more than anything, was to be returned, like a child, to the absolute care of our parents.

I imagine that one of the great difficulties of a disease like schizophrenia—which generally develops in a person's 20s or 30s—is, for many people, a loss of independence. You are trying to push forward as a fully functioning adult, but something holds you back. There is a central dynamic, then, of resistance—towards doctors, family, meds—of not wanting to let this illness box you in, limiting your chances in life. My brother, though, was different. In some essential way it always seemed to me that he had chosen, instead, to retreat back to childhood—which was, after all, one of the only safe places he had known. More than once when I was home visiting, during the last years of his life, he would ask me on the phone if I wanted to come over and play.

By then, he had cordoned off so much of the world from himself, you see, though in a sense this was hardly a sacrifice, because most of what he had turned his back on, of what he had abandoned all hope for, would never have been offered to him anyway. For our parents, near the end, it must have felt like they were losing a ten-year-old boy.

But to leave it simply at that lessens too much. It disregards so many of the things that my brother had fought to overcome. And it says nothing of the dignity with which he died; the dignity with which—I would come to see, by the end—he had lived.

〈〈〈〈〉〉〉〉

*A comic book **panel** (alternatively known as a frame or box) is one drawing on a page containing a segment of action. **Encapsulation** is the art of capturing prime moments in a story inside the layout of a page. Panels may be nonsequential or even asynchronous, spanning more than one moment in time.*

*"**Clair de Lune**" (French for "light of the moon") is the third and most famous movement of Claude Debussy's "Suite Bergamasque." It is a piano depiction of a poem by Paul Verlaine. Debussy began composing the suite around 1890, at the age of twenty-eight.*

*In comics, **sound effects** are words without bubbles that mimic sounds. They are not subtle and are often used to help depict a fight scene with a decorative "WHAM" or "BOOM."*

*Debussy wrote "Clair de Lune" in the key of D Flat, with a 9/8 meter. It is meant to be played in **pianissimo**, which is the softest dynamic in music.*

Almost everything my brother did was loud. He had a booming voice, which extended to his laughter and his cough. He was a loud chewer of food and a prodigious snorer. He preferred to listen to the television at levels that struck me as absurd, and whenever he walked through the house you knew exactly where he was. But my brother could also play Debussy in pianissimo. It did not come naturally to him, though eventually he learned. I'm not even sure when it happened—one year I came home and noticed that he was no longer indiscriminately pounding away at the keys for every piece of music. I think it was over the last years of his life, when he knew he would soon die, that he taught himself that delicacy.

In the days after my brother's death, we clean out his apartment. I suggest paying someone else to do it, but our parents insist. Our mother and I focus our attention on the kitchen, filling large bags with recycling and trash, boxing up plates and glasses for Goodwill. In the refrigerator, I count five nearly empty bottles of ketchup. Apart from perishables, my brother wasn't a fan of putting things away. The cupboards sit almost bare, while the kitchen table and counters are covered in dishes, paper towels, bags of chips and cookies, boxes of soda and cereal. There is, I'll admit, a certain logic to this—why put the things you know you will want behind closed doors? Our father walks out of the bathroom carrying two large Ziplock bags full of loose pills he has collected. "If you want me to take care of those," I offer, "I'd be happy to pass them out to the kids downtown." A soft laugh, but he turns me down. In the main room, my sister makes stacks of DVDs and bright colored fantasy books. Though our nephew is eleven years old, he and my brother shared much of the same tastes in entertainment. None of us want to be doing this, but it seems better to be doing it together.

With the kitchen more or less packed, I walk into the bedroom, where all the available surfaces are cluttered with allergy and cold medicines, loose change and dead batteries. My brother seems to have had an endless supply of blue jeans and belts. For decades he couldn't stop gaining weight, then all of the sudden he couldn't help losing it, so my brother was always in need of different clothes. In the drawer of his nightstand I find a stack of journals, and on the top shelf of his closet I find two more stacks. I have always considered myself the only writer of the family—hardly prolific, but doggedly committed all the same. Now, I count a total of twenty-four journals. Some of their covers are black, though most are pastel-colored—green, blue, purple—marketed, no doubt, for children. His nearly illegible scrawl fills up page after page. I turn to one entry and read the first few lines: "I am a nice and caring person. I am clean and innocent. I would never do something like that . . ." All day I have trusted that I could handle this, that I could help our parents sort through my brother's sad belongings—even crack a joke or two to help us all get through—but these journals are too much. I sink down on his unmade bed—the bed they had helped him out of a week before to take him to the hospital. Our father walks in and finds me there with the piles of spiral-bound notebooks. "I knew he journaled," our father says, "it was something the doctors suggested he do to calm himself down. But I didn't know he did it this much."

For reasons I can't understand, neither of our parents will want to keep these notebooks, or even crack one open, so at the end of that week, I fly back east with all twenty-four of them: a carry-on bag full of my brother's words.

Aaron's first nervous breakdown took place the month I graduated from college. His life had been spiraling out of control for most of that year, but we were slow to read the signs for what they were. After a falling out with his roommate, my brother had moved back in with our parents, and when he wasn't putting in his shift at the pizza parlor where he'd worked since high school, he stayed mostly in his room. Increasingly, he would make comments that made no sense—about cameras hidden inside walls, policemen following him home at night. Things didn't bottom out completely, however, until the summer. But I don't want to say much of that time, not here.

My plan had been to celebrate graduating with a long road and backcountry trip throughout the West, but I headed home instead, wound up staying a full year. I got a job doing data entry for an online sports apparel company, which allowed me to look after my brother during the days when our parents were at work. When my brother's condition was manageable, I'd plug pointless numbers into an Excel spreadsheet, while we watched DVDs—the first of the X-Men movies, Michael Keaton's stint as Batman, the unfortunate Star Wars prequels with Jar Jar Binks and Natalie Portman.

Over the years, we kept watching—a couple movies each time I'd visit home. We stayed away from anything too edgy or violent, and gravitated towards the characters and plotlines that we knew from childhood. Say what you will of the cinematic worth of the superhero franchises, they are at least dependable—always a new release or coming attraction for him to look forward to, for us to make plans around. After I got married and settled into a life on the opposite coast, we watched fewer movies together, though we'd still discuss them on the phone.

No one would mistake my brother for a riveting conversationalist, but he was certainly thorough—offering a twenty-minute synopsis for a two-hour film. The only times I'd ever watch such movies without my brother was when I was on a plane ride home, scrolling through the free offerings to find something we could talk about after I'd land.

Our father is at home on the couch reading a book or watching TV when the phone rings. Every weekday night my brother calls to tell him about his day at work, but this is too early for that. It is my brother's supervisor saying that Aaron cannot finish his shift, cannot gather his breath enough to even talk on the phone. My brother's supervisor is kind, is scared. He has witnessed all sorts of things with this job, but he likes my brother, who has been at Pearl Buck longer than he has. He is sorry to trouble our father, but he doesn't think Aaron should try to drive home.

It takes our father a half-hour to get my brother out the door and into the car. Takes them another half hour to get from the car into his apartment. Surely, he should take my brother directly to the hospital, our father thinks, or at least back to their place, but Aaron says he wants to sleep in his own bed. "It is just this darn asthma," he says with effort. "I'm sure I'll be better tomorrow."

In the morning, our father calls the doctor, who tells him to get Aaron over to the ER right away. A day later and I am coming home.

"It's that bad, huh?" my brother asks from his hospital bed, trying to catch our father's eye.

"No," our father answers weakly. "He just wanted to come."

I scoop the dice up with my hand, place them in the small plastic cup, and pass it to my brother. He is giving me a hard, mistrustful look or else he is absent-mindedly watching TV; he is laughing about something that only he thinks is funny or else he is on the verge of tears—in any case, he takes my offering, shakes the cup eagerly around and rolls the dice onto the carpet. We are playing Yahtzee—for the first or fifth or eleventh time of that day, of this long unfortunate night that we have no choice but to see through. You might think we are both children, but we are in our twenties or thirties. Not one or the other, but both.

For close to a decade my brother played this game every night, either with me or one of our parents. Somehow this was my idea, the red box pulled out from the back corner of a closet full of puzzles and games. The faces of the kings and jacks in a deck of cards scared him, as did—oftentimes— whatever image was on the front of my T-shirt. So we'd put the cards away and I'd turn my shirt inside out, and we'd play.

Our mother prints out hundreds of copies of the Yahtzee scorecard at her work and we burn through them at a rate you wouldn't believe. Over the years, he stops adding up his score but never stops wanting to win. The simple repeated actions—the sound of dice inside the rattled cup—soothe him, keep him out of his own crazy head. Most nights, if he can't sleep, he will wake our father to play, but if I am home—for a few nights or weeks or months—I ask him to wake me instead.

Once, during these years, I am out having a few beers with friends. One of those bars that has a large shelf of games to while away the time as you drink.

"How about a round of Yahtzee?" one of them asks on a whim.

"If you even attempt to play that game in front of me," I respond, "I will have no choice but to punch you in the face."

In a spin-off of the X-Men series called Legion, Charles Xavier—while working in a psychiatric facility as a young *man—has an affair with a patient named Gabrielle Haller. After their affair has ended, and unbeknownst to Xavier, Haller gives birth to their son, David. The central character of the series, David takes on the name of Legion after developing a severe mental illness centered around multiple personalities—a condition known more officially as **dissociative identity disorder**.*

*Fewer than one percent of Americans suffer from schizophrenia. Brain-imaging studies of patients show a rapid deterioration of **cortical gray matter**—the structural components which form the brain. Each psychotic episode causes further loss, with the patient never regaining their previous state of functioning. Due to this—at least in part—people with schizophrenia die on average twenty-five years earlier than the general population.*

*In the world of comics, **closure** is the act of mentally filling in the gaps of what we observe in individual panels—the process of making narrative sense out of mere fragments. It is the agent of change—of time and of motion—that a reader uses to create a unified reality.*

*The word "schizophrenia" was coined in 1908 by the Swiss psychiatrist Eugen Bleuler. It is a combination of the Greek roots **schizo** ("split") and **phrene** ("mind"), meant to address the "loosening of associations" that are common in the disorder. It is an illness, then, that causes an individual to get lost in the fragments, to lose track of the narrative through-line that makes sense of the world.*

*Legion is an **Omega-level** mutant—designating the most dominant in existence. He is able to absorb the mutant powers of others into his psyche. At times, Legion does this on purpose, with a clear intent in mind, though it also takes place against his will, whenever he is near someone who dies.*

***Capgras Syndrome** is a rare psychiatric disorder in which a person holds the delusion that someone close to them (generally one or more members of their immediate family) has been replaced by an identical impostor. There is no verifiable cure for the syndrome, though regular therapy, with the support of anti-psychotic drugs, can be effective.*

*In one issue of the series, a delusional Legion travels back in time, to the decade before his birth. In the middle of a struggle, he accidentally kills his father, thereby ceasing to exist. The death of Charles Xavier—one of the most central figures in the X-Men universe—creates a catastrophic alternate timeline that becomes known as the **Age of Apocalypse**.*

During multiple psychotic episodes—the most severe lasting for several weeks—my brother believed that all of his family had been replaced by evil duplicates. While my brother had no history of violence, this condition often resulted in him becoming aggressive and confrontational. My brother was never a strong man, and he had no idea how to acquire or make use of a gun, but this didn't mean there was nothing to worry about—what if you were asleep? What if he came at you with a kitchen knife or an aluminum bat? What if, God forbid, you had not yet managed to take away the keys to his car?

Envision, if you will, the paneled montage of a restaurant interior. Caption: a family dinner. Close up of a corner booth, where all is shadow and garish colors; speech bubbles with bold font.

After my first year of teaching back east, I am home again, for the summer at least. Or, what's left of it—my cross-country trip stretching to three weeks, then four, in no hurry to get here, or anywhere. Since the last time I saw my brother, he has spent more time in the psych ward and quit another job. "A complete waste of time," he told me over the phone. "Besides, I can get any job—I'm good with people."

Only he is not here tonight, by design it would seem, which isn't to say that his presence doesn't hover over the entire scene. Our mother looks exhausted, looks aged. Evidently death has been on her mind, mostly her own. "If something was to happen to the two of us," she says, fixing her eyes on me from across the table, "promise that you won't move back to take care of him."

Zoom out to a long shot: laughter and loud voices rising from the nearby tables. Our waitress clears the plates, leaving a check.

In the old D.C. and Marvel comic books, the heroes are always being forced to choose. A city bus, for instance, full of helpless New Yorkers, teetering on the edge of a blown-out bridge, or else a serial love interest—semblance of a normal life—in trouble somehow, screaming his name. The cardboard villains stand by, eating it all up.

Only if you are Clark Kent or Tony Stark, or even Peter Parker, the right choice is always both—save everyone.

"You've got to promise us" our mother says again. "We've made arrangements," our father adds. "He'll be taken care of."

I had watched such scenes play out before. I knew all my lines. I weighed all the costs.

I promised.

In the picture I keep framed on the desk in my study, my brother is only a small boy—six or seven I'd guess, though there is no way for me to be sure. Lying on his back on the brown shag carpet of our childhood home, his legs are crossed in a manner that could only be comfortable for a child. He is listening to a record on our father's turntable, plugged in with a large set of headphones—the kind that would soon drift out of fashion for several decades, then circle strangely back in. He is dressed in the type of slacks we only ever wore on holidays or for church, as well as an ugly knit sweater and a pair of bright blue sneakers with yellow stripes that I would gladly trade away fifty bucks, my stack of *X-Men* comic books, and whatever may be left of my Halloween candy, if only they could somehow fit my overgrown feet. I'd like to know what he's listening to, but the album's cover—within his reach there on the carpet—is blurred.

In this snapshot moment, as my brother gazes intently at the ceiling, I wonder what he thinks will become of his life. I wonder if, already, there is some part of him that worries none of this will work out—that the world will open up for him like an empty box, closing itself up with him inside.

I don't know which of our parents took this photograph, but I hope they had the decency to leave him there, undisturbed. That he wasn't interrupted with calls for dinner or chores, or that I didn't run in from the other room, hounding him to join me in another game. Because what I want more than anything is for him to remain right where he is—alone with his music, his thoughts—before the last song is over, before the record slows to its inevitable standstill, and the needle jerks back abruptly into place. Before the whole rough world barges in again, leading him to where he has to go next.

Grief does not become Thor—god of thunder, king of Asgard—who is, at this point in the movie, hiding out in a Norwegian fishing village for refugees. He has always been the chosen son, the wielder of an enchanted hammer that only he could lift, but now he tips back beer after beer. He plays video games and complains about the cable. The Avengers have come to this faraway place to seek his help.

"Why don't you ask the Asgardians down there, how much my help is worth?" Thor replies, still despondent after his loss in battle. "The ones that are left anyway."

Agelessness is the province, not just of the gods, but of all superheroes. Spider Man will always be juggling his schoolwork; Captain America, though he stayed asleep for seventy years, hasn't aged a day. But now Thor has a giant gut, an unkept beard. "The future hasn't been kind to you has it?" quips his long dead mother in a later scene, and in the seat beside me my brother laughs. It wouldn't be a Marvel movie, after all, without a few cheap jokes, even when so much is at stake.

As a teacher and as a writer, I know that some of the stories of our lives must be drafted and redrafted multiple times. In the hopes that, eventually, we will get the telling right, and they will leave us at peace.

When our parents asked me, inside that crowded restaurant, to promise that I would never move home to take care of my brother, the truth is that I didn't say a word. Or, rather, that I put them off. "I don't want to talk about this right now," I probably said, knowing full well that I wouldn't want to talk about it later either. Maybe you think this comes down, simply, to pride—that I thought too highly of myself to say those words aloud, and maybe, in a way, that is correct. But that is only one version of the story, and the truth is more complicated than that. The truth is that I had already made that promise to myself years before, after a particularly awful week alone with Aaron, when his delusions grew out of control. I needed to get him to the hospital, but I knew there was no way I could do this on my own and had to call in strangers to help.

Until that week, I had always thought that I could take care of my brother. Which isn't the same as saying that I always would, simply that I felt myself capable of it; that I could, when necessary, stand in for my parents. But I never believed that again afterwards. I never felt as close to him, never felt as fully at ease in his presence, or—for that matter—safe. The truth is that, after that week, I never stopped worrying about what might happen—to Aaron, to all of us. And it seemed that there was no right way I could tell our parents this version of the story, even now.

During my first night at the hospital, as my brother somehow sleeps—amid the fluorescent lights and the periodic noise of the machines—I sit in a straight-backed chair with my laptop. Even in tragedy, it turns out, there will be email. I respond to students' questions about a hastily put together assignment, send a brief update to my boss, cancel a poetry reading I was supposed to give that weekend in Tuscaloosa. For over a decade now, my brother has insisted on sleeping with the lights on, and—more often than not—the TV, so I shouldn't be surprised to hear him snore, even with the unnatural heaving of his chest and the oxygen mask strapped to his face. The night attendant is a young woman with dreadlocks. She reminds me of one of my students—only with more gravity, more attention to detail and care. I trust her, feel good that my brother is under her watch through the night. At one point, he startles himself awake, looks uneasily around the room until he sees me. "Thanks for staying," my brother says softly, then closes his eyes and drifts fitfully back asleep.

Fridging *is a comic book trope in which the love interest of a hero dies, or is otherwise cast aside, to further a male hero's story. The term comes from a storyline in the* Green Lantern *series in which a villain literally leaves the corpse of the central hero's girlfriend in a refrigerator for him to find. The term was coined to call out how lazy male writers can be in their depictions of female characters.*

Like Iron Man, Claude Debussy cycled through an array of glamorous, and oftentimes married, women in his life, casting them aside whenever it suited him. "I honestly don't know if Debussy ever loved anybody," wrote Mary Garden, who starred in **"Pelleas et Melisande,"** *Debussy's only opera. "He loved his music—and perhaps himself."*

In the early days of comics, **motion lines**, *or "zip-ribbons" as they are sometimes called, were a haphazard attempt to impose motion over a static scene. Think of the curving line that follows a swung fist, or the backdraft of a getaway car speeding off the page. Over the years, and at the hands of seasoned artists like Marvel's Jack Kirby, motion lines became more refined, taking on a style all their own.*

*Paul Verlaine was a **French Symbolist** poet—advocating for musicality over statement, and for the value of elusiveness in art. While Debussy was busy composing instrumental depictions of his poetry, Verlaine was descending into a life of drug addiction, alcoholism, and poverty. His fall was over two decades in the making, but it began in 1872 when he abandoned his wife and newborn child to run off with the teenaged poet and anti-hero Arthur Rimbaud.*

*The creation of comic books is sometimes divided into different specialties, including the **writer** who creates the story, the **penciller** who lays down the basic artwork, and the **inker** (traditionally working with India Ink) who enhances the penciled artwork.*

By the end of his life, my brother had an impressive array of doctors, including multiple oncologists and surgeons, a heart specialist, and his long-time psychiatrist. While no doubt intended as an orderly division of labor and expertise, the chief result was too often a labyrinthine endeavor to coordinate between their respective offices, with scheduled treatments, testing, and surgeries always being delayed for one reason or another. It made you feel, again, how small a part we play, even in those stories we think of as our own.

I am back in Oregon for a couple months after finishing my sophomore year at college. I've got a lousy job working nights as a hotel bell hop and become quick friends with the guy I work with. One night he invites me over to a house party at the end of our shift. This is a rougher crowd than I grew up with. For years my co-worker has put in time on the rodeo circuit, and those are the people who are there. By the time we make it over it is almost midnight, and everyone is obviously a few beers ahead of us. A guy I don't know, or at least don't recognize, calls me by name.

"You don't remember me?" he asks drunkenly. "We went to high school together for Christ's sake. I was a year ahead of you."

This is not a conversation I feel much like having, but here we are.

"Yeah," he continues, "I even worked with your brother over at Papa's Pizza for a while. We used to call him Igor because he could hardly turn his neck. How come he can't turn his neck?"

"Just born that way, I guess."

There's a small group of people around us, listening in, and I'm out of practice when it comes to this sort of thing. Where I go to college, nobody has ever even met my brother.

"Yeah, either that, or I'd call him Penis, because he sort of looks like a penis."

The girl beside him laughs.

"Clever," I reply, but I leave it at that.

"Man, get the hell out of here," my friend says. "Go get yourself another beer."

The guy looks annoyed, but he does what he's told.

That night was over twenty years ago now. You would think I'd have let this go, especially as it was hardly the first time I had failed to speak up for my brother. Should I have thrown my beer in the guy's face? Asked him to step outside?

Something, surely, other than wait for my friend to step in and tell him to fuck off.

"Sorry about that," my friend says to me later.

"Whatever," I reply, with a wave of my hand, though I leave soon afterwards.

With few exceptions, the collected and undated pages of my brother's journals consist of a single entry—copied out hundreds, maybe even a thousand times. Two-hundred-and-forty-eight words by my count, though some of them I still can't decipher, struggle to make out. "My parents are way bigger than Eugene, Oregon. They won't let me get hurt." Like a script, or a piece of sheet music he is trying to memorize, my brother stumbles through an endless series of takes. If he writes it out enough times, and with enough belief, then maybe—like a spell he will cast—the fears will go away.

My brother lived in the same apartment for the last twelve years of his life. I helped him move into that place, helped him stack all his hand-me-down furniture into the grimy kitchen, when it came time to have the carpets replaced. I have watched countless movies there, tried and failed to teach him how to make simple meals like nachos and boxed mac-and-cheese, so I can see him clearly, seated in his old La-Z-Boy chair, writing these entries.

Say it is a Sunday, which means he will have just spent the entire day at our parents'—watching TV, practicing piano, talking for hours with our father about sports, movies, and work. Always these same few topics that form my brother's world. He will have had some leftovers for lunch, asking our father, like always, how long he should microwave it for. Our mother will have made a nice dinner, after which he will watch more TV, putting off—as long as possible—the need to say goodnight and leave.

The drive back to his apartment went okay, but now he is tense. His upstairs neighbors are making noise again. He would like to turn the TV up loud enough to drown out everything else, but there have been complaints. He would like to call our parents, to help calm himself down, but he just left there. He thinks of calling his brother on the east coast, but it is too late for that, and he never has his ringer on anyway.

He opens his journal to the first open page. "I am clean and innocent," he writes. "I would never do something like that . . ." Beside him, in framed pictures on the coffee table, are his most faithful companions—my brother holding the family dog; my brother and our parents tailgating at Autzen Stadium; my brother in a half-tucked in shirt, posing with me at my wedding—together, they will make it through the long night.

My brother glances at the clock, almost 11 PM. Seven more hours till sunrise, ten more till Barnes & Noble opens and he can get his daily latte—maybe Wendy will be working, or Coleen, he knows them all by name. Fifteen more hours and he can go to work. Maybe our father will meet him for lunch again. Maybe this new treatment will actually help. He handles the chemo well, apart from the nosebleeds, but the steroids make him anxious, keep him up all night worrying like he used to—those lost years he tries not to think about. He glances at the clock again: almost midnight. Nine hours till Barnes & Noble, fourteen hours till work. My brother is crafting a suit of armor out of an infinite supply of kids' movies and Diet Cokes. He reaches again for his journal and writes out his entry—"My parents are way bigger than Eugene, Oregon"—the wild loops of his boyish cursive fill up the page.

So much of the comic book world is predicated on tragedy, on loss. Superman is the lone survivor of a doomed planet. Batman, when he is all of eight years old, witnesses his parents getting brutally murdered. By the time I got to high school, I was more drawn to the somber lives of poets than superheroes. My literary tastes may have evolved, but part of me was still seeking out the same macabre tales.

In the course syllabus that someone has most likely already designed, American superheroes get paired with famous poets. Easy enough to plot an ill-fated line between Batman and John Berryman, to begin with Wolverine and wind up with Arthur Rimbaud.

And my brother? He was never one to chase after sorrow, and I can't say with any certainty what first drew him to the tales of Gotham City and Metropolis. Perhaps it simply came down to our lives as brothers, always following one another's lead—with bunk beds and shared toys, with the same friends and a joint collection of baseball cards. When the other person's birthday was just as good as your own— the glittering line of presents, for all intents and purposes, gifted to you both.

But as we got older, I saw his fascination more clearly for what it was: a route back to childhood, the sad hope that who we were had never really changed. At his funeral, I read Czeslaw Milosz's prose poem "Christopher Robin," based on another of my brother's longtime favorites: "Owl says that immediately beyond our garden Time begins, and that it is an awfully deep well . . ."

My brother is out to lunch with a friend from Pearl Buck.

"I should probably tell you something," this friend says to him. "I'm transgender."

"That's fine," my brother says, smiling, no doubt, between bites of his sandwich, but he has no idea what this means.

That night, after getting off work, he calls our father to ask. Our father who, until recently, was a lifetime Republican, whose only brother tunes in exclusively to Fox News and is a proud member of the NRA.

"That's fine," our father says, though he too is unsure what this means. And when, after reading a few things online, he is still confused, he calls to ask me.

In another memory I am seated alone in a movie theater on Cheju Island, South Korea, watching *Crouching Tiger Hidden Dragon*.

How much orchestrally-dubbed, tree-top flying, samurai-sword-fighting am I supposed to take? I don't even know what anyone is saying (their lines spoken in Cantonese with only Korean subtitles), or if this even counts as a superhero movie, but my brother has gone missing again, and I can't go looking for him here.

Fifteen hours is the time-difference between this island and home, so that my landline leaps like an alarm in the morning or jolts me back upright at night when I am nearing sleep, knowing that it is either him or it is about him, that something has gone wrong or is about to go wrong. 2 AM back in Oregon now, and our parents have given up on finding him tonight, trying to catch a few hours of sleep. And I am here in this crowded theater, because I could no longer wait by the phone, because the afternoon heat on this island—where I have come to teach for a year—is insufferable without AC, and because this movie struck me as something that he and I would have watched together.

Up on the screen, the women are all so beautiful, in their balletic fighting poses and long flowing robes. There appears to be some sort of love angle, though I can't piece together exactly who or what. A month ago, my brother turned twenty-six. As far as I know, he has never so much as kissed another person, though in his delusions he has had all sorts of wives—movie stars and fantasy characters who we have kept from him; women whom, no doubt, he would fly away with someday soon. *Where have you disappeared to this time, brother? Are there words, if only I could translate them, that would bring you home?*

I focus back on the movie, where two of the main characters, a man and woman, have gathered on an empty bridge overlooking the chasm of a large waterfall. It is morning; there is a majestic fog. The woman says something calmly to the man, then turns away and leaps.

I am ready for this to end. We are all ready for this to end. Though some conclusions are, no doubt, more bearable than others.

The Belgian cartoonist Georges Remi, who worked under the pen name Herge, charted his own course far away from the macho fantasies of American superheroes. In The Adventures of Tintin, *Herge developed his signature **clear-line** style, offering a combination of cartoonish central characters against highly detailed and realistic backgrounds. Set in a largely authentic 20th century, Tintin's travels often take him to exotic locations throughout Asia and Africa. What the series offers its readers, then, is not so much a separate world entirely, but an escape from whatever confining one you are in.*

The **diathesis-stress model** is a psychological theory that attempts to explain a disorder by the interaction of a "predispositional vulnerability" and the stress caused by actual events. It pairs the abstract, biological or genetic trait with real life situational factors. Two individuals may be equally predisposed toward developing schizophrenia, for instance, but only one of them will reach the threshold of stress factors necessary to trigger the disorder.

In the world of superheroes, **crossovers** happen when story elements of two or more comics come together to create a storyline. The outcome of a crossover feature can affect ongoing titles for years to come, creating an intricate web of intersecting plots. The recurring battles that take place between Iron Man and fellow Avenger Captain America are one of Marvel's most famous crossovers.

The scandalous affair between Verlaine and Rimbaud spanned two years and several countries. In Belgium, July of 1873, Verlaine fell into a drunken rage and fired two shots from his pistol at his young lover, somehow managing only to wound his left wrist. For this, Rimbaud had Verlaine thrown in jail. Still just twenty years of age, Rimbaud disowns all of his poetry, joins the Dutch colonial army, and sails to the **Netherlands East Indies**—a territory that is now part of Indonesia. After a mere thirteen days, Rimbaud disappears, fleeing into the jungle.

India Ink was first invented in China, but the English term was coined due to their later trade with what was then a British colony. The carbon black from which India Ink is formulated *was obtained by burning bones, tar, pitch, and other substances. Cartoonists preferred India Ink because it was permanent and did not bleed once it dried.*

One of our family's fears when my brother began cancer treatments was that his mental health issues would resurface, spill over. For a guy who spent too much time watching Sci-Fi movies and reading fantasy books, his anxiety surrounding evil doctors and medical experiments was never far off. With few exceptions, he had always been willing to take his antipsychotic meds, and his condition, over the past several years, had been largely stable, but the prospect of my brother battling debilitating illnesses on multiple fronts hardly seemed possible.

When it comes time to leave the side of your ailing brother, you go looking for him everywhere. Or, if not him exactly, then some version of him, of who—with greater or lesser luck—he might have become.

Homeless men walking the streets at night, trapped inside their deranged soliloquies. The hunched over checkout clerk, working the graveyard shift at Walmart, mumbling your total without lifting his eyes.

Back on the island of Cheju, across from the hagwon where I worked, there was a middle-aged man who would stand for hours trying to gather the courage to cross the street. At first glance, he looked like all the other men, in his pressed slacks and button-down shirt, but when the crosswalk light would signal the others on, he would remain, growing noticeably angry at himself as the hours slipped away. Sometimes weeks would pass before he'd be there again, though I'd look for him each day from the second story window of my office— during my lunch break, or in the minutes between class.

One afternoon, when the heat was at its worst, and he had been out there for hours, I couldn't stand it any longer, and went down to bring him some iced tea. "Masida" (to drink) I said kindly in my horrible accent. At first he flinched and drew back, his shirt soaked fully in sweat. But when I reached the cup forward with two hands—the Korean gesture of offering—he took it: suddenly cheerful, gulping it down in a few long swigs, and talking so fast I couldn't catch a word he said. Then he fainted, smacking his head hard on the pavement. He came to almost at once, slapping my hands away and screaming at those of us who had gathered around him. We all stepped back and he ran off, down the block and around the corner. But he was no one's brother I knew, so I let him go.

From as far back as I can remember, my brother played the piano for several hours a day. The houses of our childhood friends—even with the TV turned on and their entire family talking at once—always struck me as oddly quiet. I wish I could claim that even as a kid I enjoyed listening to him play, but the truth is, when I wasn't outright annoyed, I was mostly indifferent. My brother was never a concert-level pianist. He never composed his own songs or made any money off of it. Once we got older, no doubt, he would sometimes practice for so long to mask the fact that he had little else to do, though playing was always something that he loved. Something that held him apart from most people, but in a way he could be proud of.

In the months after my brother's death, I often replay the video that was shown at his funeral, of his performance at Pearl Buck. Only rarely do I bring myself to actually watch it, opting instead to turn the volume up full blast and leave the room. In the breaks between songs, it is almost like I am visiting home. "Sounds good," I want to shout, pausing between the sentences of some page. Or, "I like that one, brother." He has been playing for hours. He might go on like this all day.

It has taken over half the movie, but the Avengers have finally found a way out of the world's fix. A route back or through. Something involving time travel and whatever the quantum realm is. (Luckily, suspension of disbelief is pretty much a given with these movies, so the writers don't have to dally much in terms of exposition.) This, then, is their chance at redemption—infinity within the grasp of an armored glove; the knuckles overlaid with six brightly colored stones. Somehow, it all comes down to the Incredible Hulk—or, rather, this version of the Hulk—halfway between berserker and Bruce Banner, in one of several side plots I have failed to track. "Everybody comes home" he says solemnly before donning the glove—a mantra he recites like a boy's birthday wish.

My brother gets up to use the restroom, excusing himself as he shuffles his way down the crowded aisle. I watch him grab the handrail with both hands, inching his way down the darkened steps. Even walking now is a struggle for him. If I came to his side, rose from my seat to help, would he accept? Would he take my arm? Or would we, through that simple act, only be hurrying him on towards death?

They have placed my brother on hospice. For the past two days, the doctors have administered a treatment to fight off his pneumonia—a fluid they spray in periodically through a tube in his mask that makes him panic and cough. But the treatment has not worked, and there is nothing else they can do. All the machines have been unhooked. In the morning, we will bring him home.

As our parents meet in the hallway with the hospice nurse, I try to hold my brother's scared and tired gaze. It is not the same—it is not at all the same—but I think back to his first breakdown, when we had him checked into the psych ward for a week.

Each day our parents would step into a separate room to meet with the doctor, while I'd stay with him. After we'd get home, our parents would fill me in on everything that was discussed, but for that time—for however long it would take—my job was to stay right there, to keep playing the role of younger brother. If we were kids still, I could change the subject to movies or comics. "Remember that time when

Iron Man loses everything?" I would say. "When Tony Stark was a helpless drunk living on the streets?" Only that ward was no place for children. And neither of us had any idea where we were headed next. Or who we would be once we got there.

〈〈〈〈〉〉〉〉

The comic book term **Retcon** *is short for "Retroactive Continuity." This is when a character's past is changed retroactively, sometimes to update a character. In the original 1963 Iron Man series, for instance, Tony Stark, is wounded in Vietnam, but this was "retconned" to the first Gulf War in the 1990s. This was done again in the early 2000s—for the purposes of the Iron Man movie franchise—updating the locale of Stark's formative injury to the war in Afghanistan.*

I think one way of understanding my brother's diagnosis of paranoid schizophrenia, along with his later diagnosis of **schizoaffective disorder**—*a condition that includes a combination of symptoms associated with schizophrenia and extreme mood disorders—is as a sort of retroactive continuity. A suspect attempt to make sense of the past through ascribing it with a name from the present. We use it for the ease of explanation—for the benefit, not of him, but of ourselves—to create a narrative to a plot we otherwise wouldn't understand.*

In what is often referred to as **"The Letter of the Seer,"** *the sixteen-year-old Rimbaud, writing to a friend, advocates for what he calls "the rational derangement of all the senses." This task, which requires "all his faith and superhuman strength,"* *is a reckless courting of madness; a deliberate gesture of self-destruction in the hopes of achieving lasting art. There is a level of cruelty here, to one's self, of course, but also to whomever the so-called seer makes use of or abandons along the way. Imagine the hubris of this, the certainty that whatever art you go on to make will justify all the means.*

In the 1995 crossover comic book Age of Apocalypse, *the new reality's X-Men travel back in time to the moment before Xavier's murder. There, with the help of a **psionic time loop** (think of it as a high-end crystal ball), they convince Legion of the grave damage his actions will create. In the face of this realization, Legion allows himself to be incinerated, apologizing in his final moments for all he has done.*

*Verlaine himself was hardly a sympathetic figure, and certainly he left plenty of ruins in his wake. "My soul weighs anchor for a frightful shipwreck" he wrote in his early poem **"Melancholy,"** but his theories of art still made room for other people. I think he longed for real connections in his life, and that his poetry moves away from, not towards, solipsism.*

*Legion's name calls back to a passage from scripture ("**Mark 5:9**"), in which Jesus attempts to heal a man who is deranged. "What is your name?" Jesus asks. "I am Legion," the man replies, "for we are many."*

*"I think we see our own Angel," Rimbaud wrote in "**A Season in Hell**," "and not anyone else's."*

When my brother was three years old, our parents drove him up to the big hospital in Portland to have him evaluated. The doctors said that Aaron was in the lowest percentile for boys his age, both mentally and physically, and that he would always have to deal with this. As my brother got older, the doctors warned my parents, this condition would likely manifest itself more, setting him apart from other kids.

Late at night, when my wife is away, I stream another Marvel movie, or leaf through old comic books. I'm hoping that somewhere inside this elaborate world, with its colorful sidekicks and rotating henchmen, with its glaring plot holes and skin-fitting tights, there will be a door that I can pass through—a way to feel close to someone who is gone. But I feel claustrophobic inside these bordered panels, the exclamation marks of each silly utterance. They are speaking to a boy I once or never was, and I can't manufacture an entrance back to where I want to go.

Comics are, after all, just a collection of still shots. Despite the unfolding drama, the mid-flight heroics and hackneyed sound effects, nothing ever moves, and the only real action falls inside the cracks of the paneled page; the world separated—like it always is—into what comes before and what comes after.

I leave the hospital for a couple hours to grab a bite to eat and run errands in my brother's car—adult diapers, wet wipes, a small machine that will track his breathing. While I have ridden in this car countless times, I almost always have him drive. Looking for confirmation, I guess, that he was still fit to do so. There were times, of course, when this was not possible, when I or our parents would pocket his keys for days, or even weeks—but as long as his mental health stayed in check, he drove: to work, to the movie theater, to the same handful of chain restaurants, and—almost daily— to and from our parents' house.

As you might imagine, my brother was a hesitant and highly defensive driver. He had a tendency to slam on the brakes. No matter how slow the car in front of him was going, he would not change lanes to pass. And he did not excel at parking—clipping the same pole outside his apartment dozens of times as he tried to pull into his numbered spot.

Whenever I drove with him, it was the same routine: he'd enter the car first, fasten his seatbelt, and start the engine. It could be raining; it could be twenty degrees, but he'd check his mirrors, adjust the volume of the radio (high) and the air vents (always full blast), before unlocking the passenger door to let me in.

My brother never had much chance to travel in his life, though he did make it to New York City once, right near the end. There was a trial drug that had shown early promise in treating sarcoma, so he and our father flew out in hopes of signing up. It was a difficult trip, largely a waste of time and money. For the few days they were there my brother was sick, nauseated, tired. When they met with the head doctor, they learned that the trial had been placed on hold.

"We hope to have things up and running again soon," the doctor assured them. "We will be in touch."

And they were, calling with an update, two weeks after Aaron had died.

But on their last day in the city, my brother and our father did make it out to the Statue of Liberty, as well as to the top of the Empire State Building—my brother's two requests. He texted me a picture of himself that I still have: a forced smile, a bald head, and an Oregon Ducks jacket, with the whole Manhattan skyline off in the distance. I look at it now and I wonder, how far back would you have to go to change my brother's life? Was there ever an off ramp we could have taken, to save him from what was to come? Not from cancer, but from so much else.

My brother knew the New York of paneled comic books, of the bright lights filling another Hollywood screen. Now, he finally had the chance to see it for himself.

"Mostly," our father told me afterwards, "he wished we had just stayed home."

One year, in my twenties, I lived near a public middle school, where two sisters would gather for hours on a nearby overpass that spanned an expressway. The older girl—there must have been something wrong with her—was always standing, her hands clutching at the chain-linked fence as she stared down at the polluted stream of cars, while the younger sister—maybe eleven or twelve—in what must have been a great effort of concentration or self-forgetting, would sit reading a book, her legs crossed on the dusted sidewalk.

The older girl's face was always hidden from me, her long blond hair tangled in the monotonous breeze. She must have found some solace in being there, in coming back to this place day after day. But it was the younger girl who made me take my foot off the gas each time I crested the hill, trying to interpret the expression on her face. Was she aware, already, of the tenderness that she would one day attach to this simple routine, or was she only longing for a time when she could leave all of this behind?

As I'd approach the hill each day in my car, I always made sure to have the radio turned off before they came into view. Even if I could somehow approach them, what else could I offer beyond this shared silence?

Chemotherapy is, in essence, a way to damage or stress cells that—if left undisturbed—would wreak havoc on the body. It is a poison that is administered to combat another poison, and the treatment brings with it side effects that can prove devastating.

When Tony Stark returns from Vietnam/Iraq/Afghanistan, he discovers that the shrapnel fragment lodged in his chest cannot be removed without killing him, and he is forced to wear the armor's chest plate at all times to act as a regulator for his heart. Later, Stark discovers that the **palladium** material—a rare and lustrous silvery-white metal—of the chest plate itself is slowly poisoning him, and he struggles to find a replacement.

Clozapine—one of my brother's regular medications—is considered one of the most powerful antipsychotic drugs, often proving effective in eliminating delusions. Unfortunately, the drug has also been shown to reduce white blood cell levels, making it a dangerous pairing for a patient undergoing cancer treatment.

Claude Debussy's first lawful wife, Lily, having been abandoned, shoots herself in the chest with a revolver in 1904, five days before their fifth wedding anniversary. She survives, though the bullet would remain lodged in her vertebrae for the remainder of her life. Debussy never visits her at the clinic where she is being treated, nor does he pay her bills. A popular dramatist of the day, Henry Bataille, adapts the story of the Debussys' tragic marriage into his 1908 play "**La Femme Nue.**"

Many of the side effects of chemotherapy can be traced to the damage of normal cells that divide rapidly and are thus sensitive to **anti-mitotic** drugs, including cells in the bone marrow, digestive tract, and hair follicles.

In his poetry, Rimbaud sometimes refers to Paul Verlaine as **frere pitoyable** *("my pitiful brother").*

In preparation for the surgery to remove the tumor on his lower leg, my brother undergoes his first bout with chemotherapy. Complications with his heart wind up being so severe that the doctors stop the treatment after just three rounds. When my brother loses his hair for the first time, he opts against wearing a hat whenever he goes out in public and makes regular jokes about his baldness and overall looks. Asking me more than once while I am visiting, if I have a comb he can borrow.

Our parents have left for the night. There is a new nurse on shift—an older woman who seems sweet and motherly but not as assured in her tasks as the girl with dreads. We work together to give my brother his meds. With each pill my brother coughs horribly, struggling to swallow. The nurse spoon-feeds him applesauce. "Can I chew the pills?" he asks. "You shouldn't," she replies, but it is the only way he can get them down.

My brother reaches for the nurse's hand as she readies to go.
     "What's your name?" he asks softly.
     Even then, my brother always wanted to get to know his nurses, to thank them for their kindness to him.
     "Jody," she answers, leaning over the bed so she can look him squarely in the eyes.
     "Ah," my brother mumbles through his mask, "I have a

friend named Jody."

"A good friend?" the nurse asks.

"Yes."

Since my brother's terminal diagnosis with cancer, I had—more than once—imagined myself at his funeral. Invariably I had envisioned it as a sparsely attended event, though this did not turn out to be the case. Our parents have lived in this town for close to fifty years and they had developed more genuine friendships in that time than I had realized, and the number of people who showed up from my brother's job was truly astonishing. Wholesome and ebullient-seeming middle-aged women filed in with the universal mark of educators. Many of my brother's co-workers, on the other hand, kept their heads down, as if apologizing for their very presence. These were people who had long gotten used to walking into a room unnoticed, or unwanted, and, while everything was hard for me that day, I tried my best to make them feel welcomed.

I had often viewed my brother as an imposition, so I was not prepared to hear strangers speak of him with so much affection. Over the previous week, we had reached out to his closest friends—the two or three he would meet up with on occasion for lunch or a movie. With Melissa, my brother's closest friend, I had exchanged several text messages, after our mother decided it was too hard for her. "I loved your bro so much," she wrote. "You and me we have lots to talk about." How did I not know these people as anything more than names in a tired conversation? How had I held so little interest in them? In this part of my brother's life?

I excuse myself from the table I am sitting at, and drift back to the far side of the room, where the video of my brother's recital continues to play. I find another stranger watching intently. He is alone, well-dressed, and doesn't seem part of the Pearl Buck crowd. "He is very good," the man says to me. "I didn't know he played." "Ever since we were kids," I tell him. "Our mother made all three of us take lessons, but he was the only one to stick with it." I ask for his name and recognize it at once as one of Aaron's doctors. Again, these were just names to me before, with no real existence apart from their function in my brother's life. This was the surgeon who had performed my brother's first surgery—removing most of the tumor from his lower leg. I hadn't flown home that year until after my brother was discharged. "You have to understand," the doctor tells me, "that was not an easy surgery. I did not know if we would have to amputate, or if he would ever walk again. I know your brother had many difficulties in his life, but I want to tell you that he handled that surgery with more grace and courage than most patients I work with." Grace and courage: those were two words that I had rarely thought to associate with my brother.

Part of what I am trying to say here is that I did not know Aaron well at the end. Certainly not as well as I knew him in his earlier iterations. I knew my brother as the near constant companion of my youth. I knew him as a lonely and awkward teenager. And I knew him—perhaps knew him best—as a broken and scared young man; a ruined city that I could drive away from when I needed to; a sad place on a map that I had learned to steer myself by. But perhaps my brother didn't need a time machine to salvage something from his life. Perhaps all he needed was what we all need: the chance to work through the strange and confusing phases of who we are. And, quite likely, he was much further along in that task by the end than I had ever given him credit for.

I sit in the stiff-backed chair and stare across at my brother for hours. He tosses and twists as the morphine takes hold, but he rarely opens his eyes. How bearable is this? Should we count ourselves as lucky that he at least knows who we are, that he doesn't think the doctors are trying to kill him?

I take slow walks through the wide empty corridors, wishing I could be anywhere else. After midnight in a hospital, the whole world feels haunted, or else abandoned. I keep getting chills. I want so much to leave. I see my brother's nurse in the hallway and thank her for being so patient with him. Mostly, I just want someone to talk with, to feel less alone. "Can I bring you anything?" she offers. "No," I reply. "I'm thinking I'll head home." She nods affirmatively, but something in her expression tells me I should stay.

I circle back to my brother's room but now I can't sit still, can't watch his chest uncontrollably rise and fall any longer. I'd like to walk over to take my brother's hand, but I worry that he will wake, and I will lose the will to go.

Back on the Hollywood screen, the Avengers brace themselves. After much cartoonish self-struggle, the Hulk manages to raise the armored glove and snap his fingers. He collapses in a heap—his right arm is worthless now, but he will live. And the others? The lost souls they are trying to save? The camera pans to a nearby window: birds chirping on the other side of the lifted pane; sunlight breaking through on a lone tree. A cellphone rings, a call from someone who had been lost.

Then the bombs arrive. The armada of alien ships. Something that was set right has gone back to wrong again. A turn of events both of their own making and beyond their control. The city of New York transformed into a hellscape of fire and flooding and scorched earth. "You could not live with your own failure," the resurrected villain declares. "And where has that brought you? Back to me." Now the green screens, the drawn-out sequences of battle and overblown special effects.

My brother enters from the lighted hall. He waits to catch his breath then starts up the theater's few stairs. He looks for me in the shadowed faces of strangers, but he is confused. I stand and wave.

*The Term **Off-Panel** refers to the action or narrative that takes place between the drawings that the reader sees. It is the comics version of the movie term "off-screen."*

*Somehow, near the end of his young, troubled life, Arthur Rimbaud shows up in the **Kingdom of Abyssinia** (modern day Ethiopia), where he makes a living through the trade of coffee, guns, and—most likely—enslaved people. His letters home to his sister and mother say nothing of his early escapades with either Verlaine or poetry. Instead, he speaks almost exclusively of money.*

***Stark Enterprises** is the name of the defense company that Tony Stark runs throughout the* Iron Man *series, manufacturing advanced weapons and military technologies. In* Forbes' *"25 largest fictional companies" it landed at number sixteen, with estimated sales of over 20 billion. A recurring, and rather expected, theme of the comic books involves Iron Man's struggles to keep his weapons from falling into the hands of his enemies.*

*During a military operation in World War II, following a German air raid of an Italian harbor, hundreds of people were accidentally exposed to **sulfur mustard**—a chemical agent that causes severe burning of the skin—which was being transported by Allied forces. The survivors were later found to have very low white blood cell counts, leading scientists to consider whether such an agent could have similar effects on cancer.*

*In pathology laboratories, India Ink is applied to surgically removed tissue specimens to maintain orientation and indicate **tumor resection margins**. This is the margin of apparently* *non-tumorous tissue surrounding a tumor that has been surgically removed. If cancerous cells are found at the edges of the operation it is much less likely to stay in remission.*

In December 1942, at the Yale Institute of Medicine, several people with **advanced lymphoma**—*a cancer that attacks the body's immune system—were first given a family of nitrogen mustard compounds intravenously, as opposed to breathing in the toxic elements. Their improvement, although temporary, was remarkable.*

My brother's first surgery was not successful. The chemo had shrunk the tumor in his right leg by nearly a third, but it was wrapped around the tendon of his ankle in such a fashion that it was impossible to remove entirely. The following year, a handful of tumors were detected in his right lung. A second surgery, followed by more rounds of chemo, succeeded in extracting the two largest tumors, but the others were too small to remove. Further surgeries were not feasible given my brother's deteriorating health, and as the remaining tumors continued to grow there were no more medical options available to him.

For over a decade now I have taught creative writing to undergraduates, getting paid to think out loud, to find words of encouragement for even the most floundering of students. I love my job, but it never stops feeling like an act—as if, on my way to class each day, I duck into one of the world's last remaining phone booths to don some cape.

In truth, I feel most myself now when I am alone in my study, lost in thought. With each passing year, I feel myself disappear a little more inside the books I read, the poems and essays I try to write. Except that for months after my brother dies, I stop writing and can hardly stand to open a book. That's when I start researching comics. I check out books. I take detailed notes. I search for metaphors and keep a glossary of terms. At times, it is almost as if I am with my brother again, engaged in some shared task. Only this time, I am taking the stage exactly as who I am: a lonely professor trying to say his goodbyes.

I am back from the hospital. Everyone has long been asleep. In the front room, I walk past my brother's piano—inside the small wooden bench are the stacks of sheet music none of us can play. In the family room, I see the mechanized bed with pressed white sheets where my brother will lie. Beside it, an oxygen tank. Beside that, the couch where our father intends to sleep each night until Aaron dies. In the nook, where each morning our mother reads the paper, there is an awkward lift that looks like a busted fair ride positioned next to a small commode.

Bringing my brother home had always seemed like the only permissible option, but now I am unsure. How do people do this? How do you go back to watching TV each night in the room where your child has died? What will we do the first time something goes wrong, and there is no help button on the side of the bed we can press to have a nurse come in?

Suddenly, the prospects of tomorrow—which is already today—seems impossible to face. I turn off the lights and, for one merciful moment, before my eyes can adjust, everything fades away.

One of the last things I did with my brother was watch the new trailer for *The Rise of Skywalker*. The preview had just come out and I knew he would want to see it. He was in a morphine daze—his chest still violently heaving with each labored breath—but his eyes fixed eagerly on the montage of scenes, gripping the monitor with both hands as he lifted it close. What will you think of my brother, if I tell you, in all honesty, that at that moment there was nothing more that he wanted, of what little remained of his life, than to be able to watch that movie? And what will you think of me, if I tell you, just as honestly, that in the last hours that I had to share with him, there was nothing more that I wanted than to be able to watch it with him? *Laughable*, you might say. *Maudlin*? My brother was many things by the end, but he was not easily embarrassed. And though I spent years—too many of them—feeling ashamed of the person my brother had become, I had moved well beyond that by then.

I can imagine having a different brother; after all, the world is full of them—brothers buying rounds of drinks at the bar or offering advice about girls—but I can't imagine having a different relationship with the brother that I had. And so, come the holidays, I will file in with all the others into some gaudy multiplex. I will find a seat alone towards the back, and I will stare up at all the same oddly clad characters—taking in the recycled plot twists, the familiar score. Then, this particular family saga will have ended, and I will walk out—red-eyed and brotherless—into the next stage of my life.

When death comes for one person, it hollows out so much of those who remain. It clears away the small altars that we had kept for them, sweeps clean the dusty enclaves where we once sat. As well as so many of our own illusions. The idea, for example, that we could ever be strong enough to save someone, or even manage to be there for them at the very end.

I'm awake. The shadow of our father fills the light of the doorway. "The hospital just called," he tells me. "They say Aaron is passing."

I leap out of bed, throw on the clothes I'd left on the dresser beside me. Keys in hand, I rush out into the main room where our father is leaning over in a chair to put on his shoes. Our mother is evidently still in their bedroom. "Should I wait?" I ask. He gives this a quick thought. "No," he says, "go." And I do, speeding away in my brother's car. 3 AM reads the clock on the dash; I left the hospital two hours ago.

You have to understand: I was tired. Hardly twelve hours had passed since they'd told us he was going to die. All day we had talked with doctors, nurses, hospice. Arrangements had been made. The next morning we were bringing him home.

But also this: I was scared. I was selfish. I did not want to live with the memory of being alone with my brother when he died. Because that wasn't my job. Our father's or mother's, yes, but not mine. *Thanks for staying*, he had said to me the night before, only this time I left.

I pull into the empty lot, jump from the car, and I'm running now. I'm trying to make things right. Just give us this last half hour, brother, and we will all get there in time.

The hospital lobby is so bright. As the two night-attendants break off their conversation, I feel suddenly on display.

Imagine this was your job—just another normal night shift. The man before you is breathing hard, his hair bedraggled. His voice cracks as he gives you a name. You leaf through a booklet of papers, scroll down an interminable list. You keep your eyes down, out of respect, because you know the man before you is crying now as he stands and waits. You turn another page and scroll down. You find it. You buzz him through.

*Regularly defying death is part-and-parcel of the superhero job description. Beyond the usual close calls and lethal showdowns that fill most every page, Tony Stark is once left temporarily paralyzed after being shot in the chest by a mentally unbalanced former lover; in another issue, he places himself in suspended animation and creates an entirely new artificial nervous system in order to survive; at one point in the series, he is even preserved inside something called **a pocket universe**.*

*Claude Debussy, on the other hand, died of colon cancer on March 25th, 1918, during the **German Spring Offensive** in Paris. His funeral procession made its way through the deserted streets as German artillery bombarded the city.*

***Gutters** are the unceremonious name given to the blank spaces that connect separate panels of comic books. They are a vehicle of suspense and transition; the place of both closure and the unknown.*

*Arthur Rimbaud, while still in Africa, developed a tumor on his right knee. He travelled back to France for treatment, had his leg amputated, and died—likely of **osteosarcoma**—on November 10th, 1891 at the age of thirty-seven. His younger sister, Isabelle, was at his side.*

*"To kill a man between the panels," wrote Scott McCloud in **Understanding Comics**, "is to condemn him to a thousand deaths."*

***Aaron Gardiner**—who lived his entire life in Eugene, Oregon—died, unattended, in the early morning hours of*

August 31st, 2019. He composed no great musical works and left behind no inscrutable poems.

The black inks of the Greeks and Romans were also stored in solid form before being ground and mixed for usage. Unlike India Ink, however, these formulas would wash away with water.

I stop running. The door to my brother's room is closed. The elderly nurse is there. She tells me that he is gone. I let myself in and sink down into the corner chair. He is so pale, his slack jaw is hung horribly in place. Between me and my brother's body is a distance that I don't know how to cross.

How many times had I wished him simply away? Brother pounding with his fists against a locked bedroom door, brother crying on a parking lot curb as strangers walked past . . . . That book is closed now. He can never turn back into the brother I feared. *You* have become a *he* now. Forever recast into the past tense, the third person. The close-up of a face in profile: "I remember when . . ."

Before his diagnosis and after his recovery, before the pneumonia and after another failed surgery, before the others had gotten up and long after everyone else had gone to sleep; before the medications that made his hands shake so much that he couldn't play the piano for months; before I had left again and after I had come back home—my brother was still my brother; still scared and alone; still brave and ready to laugh and filled with hope; still just a child and still far too old; still watching the same movies and still practicing Beethoven and Chopin; still dying and still wanting to live.

I don't believe there is a benevolent spirit watching over us. I don't believe in an afterlife or an in-between. But I do believe that these sentences can carve out a place for the two of us, to be brothers again, even after he is gone. Especially after he is gone, because so much of this would have been impossible to share with him otherwise.

I snap my fingers and he is here. I snap them again and he is returned to dust. Part of me wants to keep writing this forever—like a serialized fantasy propelling us forward along the same unbending track—yet another part of me is ready for this to come to a close. Not so much my brother's life and memory, but my place in it. An actor can continue to be cast in the role of some imaginary savior, long after he has stopped playing the part. And writing, after all, can slow down but never reverse time; it can delay but never replace our goodbyes.

Our parents arrive. They rush to my brother's side. They hug him and cry and take his hands. But I stay where I am. I stare out across at them as though this was all being performed on some distant stage.

"Did you get here in time?" our mother asks through her tears.

"No, Mom. No."

I don't know how long we stay like this, but eventually I sense another person in the room. It is our sister. Our parents must have called her. I haven't thought of our sister even once during this long grim night, but as soon as I look up and see her, I am glad she is here. Thankful for this last opportunity to have all five of us together in one room.

In the movies, timing is everything. There is a sequence of events—long handed down—that must be obeyed. If a hero dies, it cannot be before the war is won, the beloved or innocent child saved. The redemptive narrative is pre-ordained, and when the poignant close-up arrives, everyone has gathered to hear his throwaway last lines.

This is the storybook ending, and, no doubt, false. But some part of me still believed that if we continued to stand by my brother, to love him through all his difficulties; if we didn't apologize for him endlessly and did what we could to help him along the way, then, somehow, we would be granted this. But we ran out of time.

There, in the hospital room, I tell my family about the exchange Aaron had hours ago with the nurse. *A good friend?*

she had asked him. *Yes*. At the time, it was just another sad moment in my brother's life, but now it was, to the best of my knowledge, the last thing he ever said. "Who is Jody?" I ask, expecting her to be someone my brother knew from work. "It must be Jodi Winnop" our father answers, after a moment of thought. The Winnops were family friends from our youth. On weekends, our parents would gather to play hours of bridge, while all the kids—me and my siblings, Jodi and Ryan—would play board games or pile in together on the couch to watch TV. Each summer our families would rent a cabin together in central Oregon, where we would play for hours a game we invented called "monster hide-and-go-seek."

Before I had started middle school, the Winnops moved back east. Our parents remain close, visiting each other every couple of years, but I doubt my brother has seen Jodi more than twice since graduating from high school. For the last four years, I have actually lived in the same state as her but hadn't found the time to get in touch. For a moment, I feel sorry for my brother. I, who had always burned through the people of my life with such ease, such carelessness; who keeps in touch with no one from our childhood, or high school, and only a couple friends from college. But my brother's heart was less fickle than my own, and it didn't take much for him to consider someone a friend.

The movie ends with a scene of Tony Stark's funeral. In the final battle, he had sacrificed himself to save everyone else. That old trick.

In the run up to the drama, Stark recorded a last message for his wife and daughter, in case he never made it home. "I'm hoping if you play this back," he begins, "that it is in celebration."

The camera pans across a stoic line of familiar heroes decked out in black suits and dresses. A wreath is floated out across a still lake.

Now the lights can come on. Now the audience can hurry toward the winged exits. But my brother and I will stay in our seats. Until the crowd disperses. Until the silence between us grows heavy. Until the two of us are the only ones that remain.

"I'm so sorry for your loss," the head nurse begins, in a tone no doubt perfected over the years. She is a heavy-set, middle-aged woman who, up until now, I have only ever seen seated at the front desk. She is here to walk us through what comes next, the sequence of unavoidable steps now that he has died. We try to follow along, to play our parts, but as she talks, our mother sorts through my brother's duffle bag—the few belongings they had brought him from home. She pulls out a clean set of clothes—a T-shirt, shorts, underwear and socks, setting them down on the corner of the bed as though selecting them for the next day of school. Her fingers linger there, over the worn cotton, the simple tags. "For him to wear" she declares softly, not so much to the head nurse but to the whole room, as she lifts her eyes again to look at the wasted body of her son. "That won't be necessary ma'am," the nurse breaks in. "They won't transport him in clothes anyway." The woman turns back to our father, to something she was telling him, without giving it a further thought. But our mother's eyes are fixed on the folded shirt, the baggy shorts that once held his form. "He should be in his clothes," our mother says sharply, her voice breaking. The woman realizes too late what is happening, tries to calm her—"Of course ma'am, you can leave them"—as our mother sinks into our father's arms.

We are gathering our things. We are ready to depart. But after the others file out the door, I walk over, finally, to my brother's side, and I take his hand.

My brother loved all kinds of music, and there are dozens of works—both classical and contemporary—that will always remind me of him. Yet in the months after his death it is "Clair de Lune" that I latch onto, that I play on repeat in my car, or hear softly in my head when I am trying to sleep. I'm drawn to the sparseness of it, how the whole piece feels drowned in the pedals. As well as the simple melancholy that pervades throughout—even in its lush second movement— how it reaches up to the higher notes, towards some beauty or understanding, but also never asks for this to stay. "While singing in a minor key," wrote Verlaine in his poem, "They seem not to believe in their own happiness." Except that's not what I hear in the music, which evokes for me no sense of doubt or regret—the joy of this middle section feeling less failed than fleeting, the descent back to its earlier melody less resigned than relinquished.

I know nothing about music theory or technique, but I believe this four-and-a-half-minute piano solo contains something that I am trying to teach myself: about loss, about grief. How it ends, no doubt, in sadness, but also at peace.

One brother sits alone in a room, night after night, writing out the same entry hundreds of times. The other brother sits by himself in a different room, trying out dozens of endings. I want to claim that they are still connected somehow, that no boundary or separation is absolute . . .

We are just back from the hospital, still an hour or two before dawn. Our mother has gone to lie down, while our father—not knowing what else to do—brews the day's first pot of coffee.

Thank you for not taking them with you brother. For not going out like a rocket that one of us would have to fly into the sun. And thank you, also, for never holding it against me for having a better life.

The coffee is ready now. We each pour our first cup. There are a dozen things I should try to say to our father in this moment, but then the phone rings—our parents' landline—

startling us both. It is the hospital, or someone at the morgue, asking about the possibility of donating Aaron's eyes. "I'm very sorry to trouble you with this matter," the voice says to our father, "but there is only so much time."

Our father stares out vacantly across the small distance of his kitchen—the granite counter tops, the wooden line of cupboards. He is amazed by his own speechlessness, and at the audacity—not so much of the question—but of his need to answer it. Perhaps he is also amazed at the idea that there could still be some part of his oldest son that could be of use.

"Yes," he says finally, his hand gripping the receiver. "Of course."

ACKNOWLEDGMENTS

Small Altars would not be the book that it is without the discerning eye and generous heart of Anna Clark: thank you, my friend. I also cannot thank Ross White enough for believing in this manuscript and helping to bring it into the light. For decades of the best companionship and important feedback on an early draft of this manuscript, thanks to Isaac Kamola. And for all that and more, thanks to my wife Rose McLarney.

I am grateful to the editors and staff at Tupelo Press for selecting this manuscript and seeing it through the stages of production. I began working on this book in the winter of 2019, while staying for a week in the snowed in upper cabin of the Dutch Henry Homestead, and I am thankful—as always—to Bradley Boyden for letting me ghost back in there every now and again. Thanks also to the fine people at the Hambidge Center for the Arts, for a residency where I worked on revising this manuscript. Other readers who gave me generous feedback on the contents of these pages include Andrew Milward and Rachel Howard. And for his artistic vision, a big thanks to Colin Sutherland.

For all they did for my brother over the last ten years of his life, and for all they continue to do for the community of Eugene, Oregon, thanks to everyone affiliated with the Pearl Buck Center—especially Margaret Theisen, Molly Kennedy, and Justin Stafford. Scott McCloud's *Understanding Comics* and Esmé Weijun Wang's *The Collected Schizophrenias* were both valuable sources for the book's glossary of terms sections. All movie quotes are from *Avengers: Endgame*.

Finally, my love and gratitude to everyone in my family— including, most of all, my brother Aaron: Even Dead, You're The Hero.

ABOUT THE AUTHOR

Justin Gardiner's books include *Beneath the Shadow: Legacy and Longing in the Antarctic*, as well as the poetry collection *Naming the Lifeboat*. In 2012-2013, Justin served as the Margery Davis Boyden Wilderness Writing Fellow, sponsored by PEN Northwest. He is also the recipient of a Faulkner-Wisdom Gold Medal for Nonfiction and the Larry Levis Post-Graduate Award from the MFA Program for Writers at Warren Wilson College. Justin's essays and poetry have appeared in journals that include *Blackbird*, *The Missouri Review*, *Quarterly West*, and *Catamaran*. He is an Associate Professor at Auburn University, as well as the nonfiction editor of *The Southern Humanities Review*.

Made in United States
North Haven, CT
27 March 2024

50546127R00050